HOW DID IT COME TO THIS?

ROBERT EDWARD BURLEY

Ordering Information:

Prime Seven Media
518 Landmann St.
Tomah City, WI 54660

Printed in the United States of America

Yuri crouched nervously in the trench as the heavy artillery barrage continued all around him. A round exploded with a deafening roar a hundred metres along the line of the fortification. Soldiers who survived the impact screamed out in agony as limbs were blown off.

They yelled for medical assistance, but no medics would come as there was no-one to support them. They were on their own. They were out of ammunition, rations and hope. Soon, the Ukrainians would arrive in their NATO supplied Humvees and take them as prisoners.

"At least when I am captured, I'll be fed and given somewhere warm to sleep," he thought to himself. He wished that he could disappear deeper into the mud in the bottom of the trench to escape the relentless shelling. Eventually the pounding abated and all he could hear was the pitiful cries of the wounded and dying.

Silence came as night descended over the battlefield. He thought he was going to die as he looked at the body of his comrade, Josef, lying in a contorted pose nearby. Josef had been hit by shrapnel and died earlier in the onslaught. Yuri reached for his bottle of vodka and swallowed a good mouthful. It warmed him a little, but he felt his nose and fingers beginning to freeze. He pulled down his woollen Balaklava and removed Josef's gloves and put them on his own hands. Then he wrapped a woollen blanket around his shoulders and crept to a dry part of the trench and huddled up out of the breeze.

He'd abandoned his Kalashnikov somewhere early in the barrage as he dived for cover and placed his hands over his ears. The cold crept into his bones and his mind began to wander. As he huddled in the trench his mind took him back to another place and time.

"I'm going down to the store Elena, is there anything you would like me to bring back?" he asked.

"We need bread, milk and some meat to cook. There's housekeeping money in the jar on the mantelpiece.

"You'd better be quick there are some soldiers checking papers," she said.

"I'll be back soon Honey," he said blowing her a kiss.

He made his way down the stairs from the Moscow apartment where they'd been living since they were married two years earlier. It was only a short walk to the store, and he felt good to be out in the fresh evening air. But when he arrived, there were lots of empty shelves due to the Western sanctions imposed when Russia had launched its 'special military operation' against Ukraine. President Putin had recently announced a 'partial mobilzation' to provide three-hundred thousand fresh soldiers for the exercise that had not been referred to as a 'war.' In fact, anyone referring to it as a 'war' could be sent to prison for ten years.

Yuri lined up and was fortunate to obtain the groceries he needed without delay.

As he walked back home, he thought about the situation. He found it difficult to believe that Zelensky, the comedian he had laughed at on television for years was now opposing Vladimir Putin and all of Russia in a war. How was Zelensky elected President of Ukraine? Putin had announced that it would only take three days for Russia to conquer Kyiv but hadn't anticipated such determined opposition from the Ukrainian people and was now entangled in a long battle for supremacy, punctuated by Russian defeats and all manner of support from NATO and the West for Ukraine. Rather than splintering NATO as he'd expected, Putin's actions had united them in a way that nothing else could have.

When Yuri opened the door to his apartment, he sensed that something was amiss. He saw Elena sitting on the lounge crying. He put the groceries on the table and went to her.

"Whatever's wrong Darling?"

"What has upset you?" he asked.

Between sobs she related that two military policemen had come to the apartment while he was away and served 'mobilization' papers for him to be conscripted into the army. She handed them to him, and he read them.

"Report to the Stalin Street Cultural Recruiting Office by 0800 on Tuesday of this week. You will be joining the President's Special

Military Operation in Ukraine to denazify the Ukrainian traitors. You should feel privileged to serve the Motherland like your grandfathers did in WW2. If you fail to report, you will be apprehended and sent to prison for not less than ten years."

Yuri's heart sank. He didn't care about Putin's 'special operation,' while he could still get on with his life as a teacher, living here with his wife, but as for fighting in Ukraine, this was a complete shock for him.

"Oh Yuri. What are we going to do. I don't want you to go away in the army. I want to have our baby. You might get killed or wounded," she cried.

"We might have to leave Moscow. I've heard that some of my friends have taken off and driven to Latvia or Finland to escape the mobilization," he told her.

"We could go up and stay with Grandfather Peter in the Ural Mountains. It's cold but very isolated and you'll be safe there until all this is over. Grandfather has a warm log cabin up there and we'll be comfortable. Grandfather will let us stay with him," said Elena.

Two hours later they had their clothes packed, along with some of Yuri's cherished books and climbed into their SUV and headed off towards the Volga on their way to Kazan.

As they approached the big, modern bridge a checkpoint guard waved them over to check their papers and asked them where they were going.

Yuri kept his cool and told them they were going to the mountains to visit Elana's grandfather who had been ill recently. The soldiers checked Yuri's name against a long list and decided to wave them through.

"That was close," said Yuri, "My name mustn't be on the list yet. I only received my call up papers in the last twenty-four hours."

Elena was trembling with fear.

"Don't worry, we'll be okay," he reassured her.

They drove on through the night and made good time until Yuri had to stop at a roadside stop and put snow chains on his wheels.

The higher up into the mountains they drove, the colder it became, and they wore their snow gear. Yuri thought that Elena looked cute in her beanie and parka.

As the sun began to rise over the Urals, they were only ten kilometres from Perm. Soon after they arrived in the mountain town they stopped and waited for the store to open so that they could buy some groceries and replenish their fuel. Elena was happy to get out and stretch her legs as they'd been sitting down for most of the night. Neither of them had slept a wink. Elena set about selecting the groceries while Yuri topped up the fuel.

When he tried to pay with his VISA card the proprietor told him that, due to sanctions imposed by the West, he'd have to pay in rubles. Fortunately, Elena had a sufficient amount to cover their purchases and paid the man without a problem.

"What brings you to these parts. I haven't seen you before?" he asked Yuri.

"We've come to visit my wife's grandfather who lives up on the old logging road," Yuri told him.

"Be careful young man that road gets very slippery when it snows and you could slide off the mountain side," he cautioned.

"Thanks for the advice. I'll drive very carefully, and we'll see you in a few days to get some more supplies," said Yuri.

"Spasibo!" he called as he left, carrying the bags for Elena.

They climbed into the SUV and were about to drive off when the storekeeper came out and called to them.

"Comrade, be careful of the brown bears. They're big and scary and they'll sometimes attack you. Just keep an eye on them if you happen to get out of your car. Remember to roll up your windows," he advised.

"Once again comrade, spasibo," said Yuri.

They did see a few brown bears as they drove up the mountain, but they were busy lumbering along pulling bark off fallen trees to search for beetles and grubs to eat.

"How far along this road is Grandfather Peter's cabin?" asked Yuri.

"Not too far now, but it all looks so different when it's covered with deep snow," she said.

Yuri glanced at the thermometer on the dashboard, and it read -6 degrees Celsius.

"It's getting colder," he said, pulling on his fur lined gloves.

Elena put on her gloves as well and pulled her parka hood down over her ears.

"Hold on. There it is Yuri. I can see smoke rising up from the chimney of the log cabin in a grove at the side of the road," she said excitedly.

Beside the cabin stood a large man in a checked flannelette shirt with braces, chopping wood next to a stack of logs. He had a bushy grey beard and wore a pair of black, rubber boots. On his head he wore a red, woollen beanie.

When he saw Yuri and Elena drive up in their SUV, he stopped chopping and placed his foot on a stump, took out his pipe, and lit it.

He was quite surprised by their sudden appearance but smiled when he realised it was his beautiful granddaughter and her husband. He'd had no visitors for months.

"Well, I'll be blowed, it's little Elena and Yuri," he exclaimed, "I haven't seen you for two years."

She stumbled to him through the thick snow and hugged and kissed him on both cheeks in the customary manner. Yuri came up to him and also hugged him. He was family.

"Come inside children and warm yourselves by the fire," he invited.

He made them a hot cup of strong coffee and passed Yuri a glass of vodka.

They all sat around the fire and Elena began to peel off her parka, jumper and woollen cap. They told Grandfather Peter why they had decided to leave Moscow and the reason why they wanted to stay with him up in the mountains.

"I don't get much news on television up here in the Urals, but I do hear on my short wave radio, that Putin's army is getting a whipping from that former clown, Zelensky. Ukrainians are our brothers. Together we fought off the Nazis and sent them scampering back to Germany. Why would Putin want to invade Ukraine?" he asked them.

"We have lost thousands of our young men already and he wants to call up three-hundred thousand more. You may stay here as long as you like Yuri, but I'll expect you to help with the animals. I've got some cows and goats and a few reindeer. You'll have to help chop and carry wood. Life up here is harder than in the city," he said.

"I'll do my very best Grandfather," said Yuri.

"We've got some provisions in our car and some of clothes. I'll go out and bring them in," he told them.

That night the chilly wind whistled through the cabin, but the small family was safe and warm inside. Elena cuddled up to Yuri, while Grandfather Peter snored peacefully in the next room. Several times during the night the old man got up to answer nature's call. On each occasion he stoked the fire and rolled on another log to keep it burning.

When they awoke the next morning, the snow had ceased, and the sun was shining. The forest all around them looked like a wonderland. The wind had abated, and Grandfather Peter was out in the shed beside the cabin milking the cows. Yuri got up and dressed and went to see if he could assist.

"Have you ever milked a cow before Yuri?" asked Grandfather.

"No I only got milk from a carton at the store," he answered.

"Well pull up that stool and I'll teach you," he said.

He followed Peter's lead.

"It's harder than it looks," said Yuri.

"Come on, try again and increase the pressure as you work your fingers down the teat," he said.

To Yuri's delight a squirt of milk spurted into the bucket.

"Now you've got it, just keep doing that," said Peter.

"How do I know when to stop milking?" asked Yuri.

"When the milk stops coming out," he answered.

Elena, who had been watching smiled as she watched them. She'd had to revise her cooking skills and was soon baking bread, cakes, biscuits and pies. Not only was she good at baking on the old fuel stove, it tasted good as well.

One frosty morning a few days later Grandfather Peter got Yuri up early and told him they'd go out and hunt for a deer to provide meat for themselves.

Grandfather took his rifle and a packet of bullets and told Yuri to strap on his snowshoes, and wear his jacket and gloves. The snow was deep on the ground but Peter led Yuri expertly to a little vale in the forest about a kilometre from the cabin. Then he showed him how to set up a hide and wait.

It was freezing as they waited but they remained quiet and very still. They didn't move or speak. After about an hour, a big buck reindeer came through the trees sniffing the breeze then knocking some moss from fallen trees and eating it.

Peter took careful aim at the buck who was breathing misty vapor breaths into the chilled air. A shot rang out like a huge explosion in the forest. The buck crashed to the ground instantly from Grandfather's headshot.

Twenty minutes later Peter had it skilfully gutted and skinned, ready to be carried back to the cabin. They tied the buck's legs to a straight pole and shouldered the load.

"The wolves will take care of the offal," said Peter.

"Wolves?" asked Yuri.

"That's what you hear outside the cabin at night, sniffing around for scraps," said Peter.

Elena was delighted by the success of the hunt. She'd seen Grandfather in action before and she appreciated that he was a skilful hunter.

Yuri was amazed at the extent of Peter's skills.

Gradually life settled down to a comfortable pace in the little cabin in the Urals. At night, before the big fire, Grandfather played Russian folk songs on his ancient balalaika. His voice was deep and resonant and told of years gone by.

"You know children, we lost twenty-seven million people during World War II to the Nazis, starvation and disease. People were eating dogs, horses and anything they could get. Many perished. Some desperate individuals resorted to cannibalism when food became so scarce. But gradually we fought them back to Berlin where that villain, Hitler, took the cowards way out and killed himself, rather than face his retribution.

Grandfather Peter did not dwell on the war. Rather, he told them how he had come to the Ural Mountains and built the cabin himself. He'd cut timber and raised cattle and battled with the wolves who came to visit to look for scraps and offal he left out for them. He confessed that they weren't to be trusted. He never left the cabin to go out into the forest without his rifle and ammunition. That gave him the edge.

He traded his tanned animal skins to make some rubles. He always kept an ample supply of vodka on hand to keep the cold away.

After four weeks Yuri decided to take Grandfather down to Perm to buy some groceries. Elena remained in the cabin and fed the cattle. Yuri felt good to be able to assist Grandfather to load the skins and get them down to the tannery.

But, when they arrived at the town, time finally caught up with Yuri. He was struck on the head from behind. Two beefy soldiers carried him back to a van and threw him into it. The mobilization police had traced his whereabouts. Grandfather was in the store and hadn't witnessed what had transpired.

When he came out to look for Yuri, he had no idea what had happened to him.

"The bastards have got him, Elena is going to be devastated," he thought.

Hours later Yuri regained consciousness. He had a splitting headache from the knock to his head and bouncing around on the floor of the van. There were no seats and where the road was rough, it was an uncomfortable ride all the way back to Moscow.

As they approached the city, three young men were unceremoniously thrown into the back of the van with Yuri. They were all runaways.

One young man said,

"I can't go to war. I'm a dental student. I don't know the first thing about weapons.'

Another young fellow said,

"I have a notion that you're soon going to be finding out."

The third man had his head in his hands, sobbing,

"I don't want to die. I'm a guitarist in a band with my friends," he whimpered.

The speeding van came to a sudden stop, and they all slid forward crashing into each other. The back door sprung open, and the big MP yelled,

"Okay you bunch of yellow-bellied cowards, get out and line up against the wall."

One young fellow asked, "Where?" and received a whack across his ear that knocked him completely over.

The other three jumped out of the van and lined up against the wall.

"You have all been called up to fight for the Motherland. If you refuse, you will be sent to prison, or shot!" the MP announced. "This is no joke. You fight or you die."

They were marched to a Q-Store and issued with uniforms, boots and greatcoats from WWII. They were ordered to dress into them.

"Tomorrow at 0600 hours your military training will commence."

The young man continued to sob, and the NCO approached him.

"Shut up Goldilocks. You'll soon have something to cry about when you get a Ukrainian's bayonet shoved up your rear! You've got to toughen up or perish!" he yelled.

Yuri's head began to spin, and his eyes became blurry. He felt his legs collapsing under him. His head was aching, and he blacked out.

He woke up in the military hospital. His head was pounding, and he was disoriented. Where was Elena? This wasn't their apartment, where was he? He drifted back into a fitful sleep.

Eventually he awoke to the sound of a trolley and the smell of food. He gradually regained consciousness, but the bright lights were hurting his eyes.

"You've decided to join the land of the living, have you?" asked the nurse.

"Would you like something to eat?" she asked.

"Here I'll help you to sit up," she said, placing a pillow behind his back.

"Where am I nurse?" he asked in a mumbling voice.

"You're in a military hospital in Moscow. You've had a nasty concussion. Your doctor will be around later, and he'll tell you more," she told him.

She brought him a small plastic bowl of soup. It felt good on his parched throat. It was chicken, and it revived him a little.

When the doctor finally came around, he told Yuri that his skull had not been fractured but the blow had concussed him badly.

"You should begin feeling better in a few days, but I don't want you up and walking around just yet," the doctor advised.

One week later he found himself back at the barracks preparing to commence his military training.

"Today!" yelled the NCO, "We are going to teach you how to fire an AK-47, so don't forget to insert your ear plugs before firing."

Yuri and the other recruits were issued with a rifle and twenty rounds of ammunition prior to lining up near the firing mound.

He ordered, "Keep your weapons pointed down range at all times. I don't want anyone turning around and pointing them back this way. If you can't keep this simple rule, I'll kick your backside until your eyes pop out."

They loaded their magazines and were assigned firing lanes. At the target end of each lane was a plywood shape of a soldier with a paper bullseye pasted on its chest.

"First shot is 'standing,' don't fire until you are ordered," he yelled.

"Take aim!" he yelled, and the recruits took aim.

"Fire when ready, one shot," he ordered.

A volley of loud reports sounded as they fired.

Yuri fired and felt the rifle jerk back into his shoulder. He'd been instructed to hold it firmly and had leaned into the shot. The spent cartridge ejected from the weapon.

"Right! Now your next firing position is 'kneeling,' position," he signalled.

Once again, he ordered,

"Take aim, fire when ready!"

They could barely make out what he was saying as they were wearing their ear plugs. They fired.

This went on until all twenty rounds were expended. Standing, kneeling, laying down and crouching. During a lull the NCO explained how to clear a bullet jam and stressed the importance of cleaning and maintenance.

At the conclusion of the training with rifles, the recruits were instructed to pick up all of the expended bullet cartridges, then take them back to the trucks in bags to be recycled.

"Yuri. Where do you think they'll send us next week?" asked his fellow recruit Sergei.

"My guess is somewhere in eastern Ukraine. They've all been talking about it. It's very dangerous they say. Already many of our Russian soldiers have been killed or wounded fighting there," he replied.

"My friend Stefan was killed last month when the Ukrainians recaptured a small village near Kyiv," said Sergei.

"I'm sad to hear that. That's terrible. This bloody war is taking too many lives on both sides. I can't understand why they couldn't have left things as they were," said Yuri.

"Many people want to know just that," said Sergei.

"The President said that he did it to prevent NATO from absorbing Ukraine but all he has achieved is to galvanise NATO and the West to unite behind Ukraine and make things worse," said Yuri.

"Sh! Don't let them hear you. You'll end up in prison for dissent," warned Sergei.

Elena looked up as Grandfather Peter drove the SUV into the yard and up to the cabin.

"Where's Yuri, Grandfather?" she asked desperately.

"The military police were in town, and they took him away in an army van. There was nothing I could do. It was probably the guard at the checkpoint that turned him in. They have probably taken him back to Moscow to recruit him into the army," said Grandfather.

"Oh no, Grandfather. What are we going to do?" she said.

"There is not much we can do, but pray that he doesn't get killed or injured," he said.

"Grandfather, I'm pregnant. Not very far along but I'm sure I am," she told him.

"Elena you can stay with me. When your time comes, Sister Maria from the village can come up and assist you with the birth, or I can drive you down there," he reassured her.

"Yuri doesn't even know that he's going to be a father," she told him, beginning to cry.

Milo reloaded his rifle and crouched in the bushes beside a blazing Russian tank with a big 'Z' spray painted on its side. The Russian occupants tumbled out of the hatch onto the snow-covered ground.

"Raise your arms! Your war is over!" he shouted.

But the three soldiers were too badly injured to comply. Milo called on the radio for medical assistance. Four other Ukrainian soldiers emerged with weapons raised and blue and yellow tape on their helmets.

They went to the assistance of the captured troops and began to administer first aid to two of them but, the third had died. Milo was becoming accustomed to this scenario and had seen too much death and injury, but it still affected him. A missile had struck the tank and it had been destroyed along with the crew inside it. The turret hung haphazardly at a strange unnatural angle.

The conscious Russian soldiers pleaded for mercy and appeared to be very young. Milo couldn't help but pity them and helped them into a more comfortable position. Then he thought, 'these soldiers had shown no mercy towards the innocent civilians they had fired upon. But they were fellow human beings and he thought that being cruel would not bring back those who had been murdered.'

These Russian soldiers could be exchanged for Ukrainian prisoners, so in that way, they were more useful alive than dead.

A Ukrainian truck soon arrived and collected the prisoners. At least they would be fed and kept warm, more than they afforded the civilians they had attacked.

Milo moved back into the forest to rendezvous with his little battle unit who were concealed in a little cottage. Boris had a stew cooking on the fuel stove and Milo was able to tuck into a large plateful with some home-cooked bread.

"What happened out there today, Milo?" asked Boris.

"I came across a blown up 'Z' tank. Two Russian soldiers were killed. One died inside and one made it out. But he died of his burns. We captured the other two who were wounded, and the truck picked them up to take them to detention to be swapped for some of our guys," related Milo.

"What stopped the tank?" asked Boris.

"A missile, a HIMARS. I suppose. It must have been spotted by a drone and those things don't miss. I'm sure glad we've got them," said Milo.

Milo was a university student before the war, studying Economics in Kyiv. Now he was a Ukrainian soldier, fighting for freedom. He found himself being sent to Bakhmut to help repel the Wagner group forces.

It was here that he came across an unfortunate young Russian soldier.

He was almost frozen to death, huddled in the bottom of a muddy trench. He set about administering first aid to treat the poor fellow who was quivering and shivering uncontrollably. Milo administered a small shot of morphine and helped him out of the wet, muddy trench.

It was Yuri. He was so cold he couldn't actually speak coherently but he managed to nod, "Thank you!"

Milo erected a small field tent to guard against the snow and dragged Yuri inside. Then he lit his camp stove to make himself and Yuri a hot coffee and a meal. Gradually the feeling began to come back into his extremities.

Finally, he stopped shaking and thawed out. He was exhausted and still quite shell-shocked from the day's artillery bombardment. Milo spoke Russian fluently so they were able to converse freely.

"I thank you for saving my life comrade. What is your name?" asked Yuri.

"My name is Milosovic, but everyone calls me Milo. I am a Ukrainian soldier," said Milo.

"I am not in favour of this war. I was conscripted to fight or go to prison. I ran away with my wife Elena to stay at her grandfather's cabin in the Ural Mountains, until they knocked me on the head, threw me into a van and sent me off to the war," Yuri explained.

"Well, my friend Yuri, your war is over for now. I'll take you to a detention centre where they'll swap you for one of our guys," said Milo.

At that moment a huge explosion rocked the forest and they both dived onto the ground and covered their ears.

"Don't panic Yuri. It's just some of your guys sending drones into the area. We are more likely to be hit by accident than by lethal intent," said Milo.

Over the following few days the two become much closer and discussed the war and the way it was proceeding.

"I really need to get back to the Ural Mountains, to my Elena and Grandfather Peter," he told Milo.

"I don't want to fight," said Yuri.

"I can't let you go Yuri. You might meet up your Russian soldiers and keep attacking us. As you said, they forced you fight. They might force you to fight us again," said Milo.

"I don't want to fight I told you," said Yuri.

But fight he did, when they were attacked by a Russian squad.

Yuri said, "Throw me a rifle and I'll help you fight them off."

Milo threw him an AK-47 and the two of them fought furiously and soon the five-man Russian squad retreated into the forest carrying a wounded comrade with them as they went.

Yuri went to hand the rifle back to Milo, but he said,

"Keep it man, it might come in handy, but don't shoot me with it."

"How could I shoot you. I owe my life to you," said Yuri.

They walked for two days in the forest avoiding roads and villages.

Yuri was surprised to see Milo pull out a mobile phone, climb a tree and speak to his parents in Kyiv.

"Yes Mama I'm okay, still having a crack at the Russians. I'm operating alone at present but not encountering much opposition. You stay well and remember to go to the subway if the missiles come over."

When Milo climbed down from the tree Yuri asked him,

"Could I try and call my wife Elena?"

"I can't promise we'll get through but we can try," he answered handing the phone to Yuri.

Yuri climbed the tree and dialled her number. At first he only picked up static but then he recognised his dear wife Elena's voice saying,

"Hello, who is it? Hello?"

Then as if by miracle it cleared up,

"Hello Elena, it's Yuri. I'm alive, I'm in Ukraine, A Ukrainian guy called Milo saved my life and we're getting by okay," he told her.

"Yuri, listen," she told him, "I'm pregnant. You're going to be a father."

Then the reception failed, and the connection ended.

"Guess what Milo, I'm going to be a father!"

"Congratulations!" said Milo.

Yuri had a big grin on his face when he told Milo the news.

They put on some coffee and cooked some rations. During the late afternoon they came across a cottage deep in the forest. When they approached a very tall old man with a shotgun pointed at them came out.

"Russians!" he commented.

"Ukrainians! Called Milo pointing to the yellow and blue insignia on his sleeve.

"What about him?" asked the tall man.

"Friendly, no problem!" called Milo.

"Okay come in, but no trouble," he told them.

An old lady peeped out of the doorway behind him. Pointing to himself, he said,

"I am Nicholas. This is my wife Vaya. Welcome."

"Come in we are just about to have dinner. You are welcome here. Anyone who fights for Ukraine is a friend of ours," he said.

The inside of the cottage was small but comfortably warm and Vaya showed them where they could sit while she served borsch from a big saucepan on the stove. She also gave them each a large freshly baked bread roll.

"Have you seen any action around here lately," asked Nicholas.

"Five days ago, I saw a Russian tank blown up by a missile. We captured two soldiers and sent them to detention," explained Milo.

"Who's this fellow you have with you? He is dressed in a Russian uniform," asked Nicholas.

"He's on our side. He's against the war. They forced him to fight and he doesn't want to kill people. His wife is pregnant, and he wants to get back to her."

"Nobody wants this bloody war except Putin," said Vaya.

"You poor young man, how are you going to get all the way back there?"

"I don't know Mam. I pray God will help me somehow. I was dying in a trench and freezing when he sent Milo to save my life. I am very fortunate to still be alive," Yuri told them.

"You certainly are young man," said Vaya.

"What are you two going to do next?" asked Nicholas.

"I must get back my unit in Bakhmut by next week or they'll think I've been killed. I think Yuri will start making his way back to his wife," answered Milo.

"This borsch is beautiful Vaya. Just like my mother used to cook," said Yuri.

"I'll second that," said Milo.

Nicholas and Vaya gave them some loaves she had baked and some coffee in a jar then wished them luck.

Back in the forest they encountered a Russian patrol, but cleverly, Yuri pretended that Milo was his Ukrainian prisoner. Yuri carried Milo's rifle and luckily the inexperienced NCO accepted the ruse and let them go.

"That was close Yuri. You lied beautifully," said Milo.

"Admittedly that fellow wasn't too bright. He was more concerned with saving his own skin," said Yuri.

Eventually, Milo had to go back and join up with his unit and Yuri had to go on his way.

"When this stupid war is over we'll get back together again and have a vodka or two," said Milo, writing his Kyiv address on a piece of note paper."

"Thank you for everything comrade," said Yuri, giving his friend a hug.

"God go with you Milo," said Yuri.

"And with you too!" answered Milo.

It was a sad parting and Yuri was quite overwhelmed by the enormity of the gigantic task ahead of him.

He headed north and concocted a story that he was heading back to his unit.

Walking along and confronting the endless wind and cold cut through and exhausted him. He kept to the secondary roads and hid, camouflaged in the forest if he encountered any Russian or Ukrainian patrols.

Fortune smiled upon him once more and he was delighted to discover a small 150 cc motorcycle hidden under a cover in a deserted farm barn. He topped up the fuel tank with two stroke petrol and tried to kick it over. It began to idle, but very roughly. He stopped it and cleaned the single spark plug and re-inserted and tightened it. This time the little motor performed beautifully.

It had all-terrain tyres fitted so he could ride it off road and through the snow easily.

Meanwhile the Russian-Ukraine conflict raged on. Eventually Ukraine began to drive some of the Russian forces back and even sent destructive drones successfully into Russia itself. NATO and the West were donating billions of dollars and Euros to assist President Zelensky to defend Ukraine against Russia.

President Zelensky visited US President Joe Biden in Washington, and he received a standing ovation on the floor of Congress as President Biden donated even greater support to help defeat the invaders. President Biden also donated the Patriot ani-missile system to help protect Ukraine.

Yuri sat staring into the fire drinking hot cocoa. Elena was cuddled up beside him on the sofa.

"Was it bad out there in the war Yuri?"

"Terrible. Unbelievable. The explosions and all that shelling is like Hell. I witnessed my comrades getting killed all around me and expected to be hit at any time. It was shocking. The noise and the smell as we cringed deeper into the mud was very hard to endure," he replied.

"How did you survive?" she asked.

"I was very lucky. I lay face down in the bottom of my trench and fortunately none of the shrapnel hit me. I was spattered with mud from the explosions," he told her, "I remained there until darkness came and I was chilled to the bone and shaking profusely, when a Ukrainian soldier, Milo found me and took pity on me and saved my life.

"He was supposed to be my enemy but saved me from dying of hypothermia and spared my life," he concluded.

"I'm glad that you met that particular Ukrainian soldier rather than another one that wanted to kill you," she said.

"Milo and I actually fought off a group of Russian soldiers together. We're real comrades now," he told her.

Grandfather Peter, who had been quietly sipping his cocoa said, "During WWII against the Nazis the Ukrainians fought beside us to kick the Germans out of the Soviet Union. I've always regarded them as our brothers. That's why I can't understand President Putin's, 'Special Military Operation,' and invasion of Ukraine. Ukraine has never attacked us. I just don't understand it."

"Vladimir Putin thinks that NATO is using Ukraine to set up an invasion of Russia," explained Yuri.

"There's no reason for NATO to invade us. None that I can think of. This war is costing Russia billions of rubles in equipment and ammunition. It just doesn't make sense," explained Peter.

"Sense or not, it's happening Peter and there's talk of an even greater mobilization to call up anyone who can fire a weapon to send to Ukraine," said Yuri.

"What if they come for you again Yuri?" asked Grandfather Peter.

"They think I'm dead. I put my dog tags on the dead Russian soldier and buried his. They'll think it's me that got killed and take me off their conscription list," said Yuri.

"I won't go into Perm for supplies so they won't see me. You seem to handle the SUV pretty well. I'll give you some money we have, to buy essentials.

It was warm by the fire, and soon they were all nodding off to sleep. Finally, Elena said,

"Time for bed. Give me your mugs and I'll wash them before I turn in."

That night Yuri was going off to sleep beside his lovely wife. She snuggled up alongside and listened to the owl outside in the tree beside the cabin.

Yuri thought to himself, "What a lovely, peaceful life is possible, preferring this to freezing in a muddy trench in Ukraine."

The new day brought fresh snow and the temperature outside dropped to minus ten degrees. Yuri and Grandfather Peter brought in some logs of wood and stoked the big fire.

Elena was already cooking eggs for breakfast and toasting some large slices of bread. The breakfast aroma pervaded the cabin. Yuri and Elena were feeling happy and content.

Milo, in the forest outside Bakhmut made it to his battle group. They were glad to see him when he checked in with the NCO. They'd believed he'd been killed in action.

"Where have you been Milo, on holidays?" they asked.

"Yes Boss. You can see I've got a lovely suntan. I've had to walk back, dodging Russian patrols because someone else took the truck and came back," he joked.

"Well, you're here now. Have you got anything useful to report?" he asked.

"Yes, there's a big concentration of Russian soldiers and two tanks hightailing it out of Bakhmut. They look like they've had their fill of fighting. From what I could learn they're mainly conscripts, and they don't know how to fight. As soon as the shelling commenced, they ran off in all directions," he related.

"Let's hope that they keep running until they get back to Moscow," said the NCO.

"They're low on ammunition and rations and they're literally freezing to death," said Milo.

"It's not too bloody warm here either comrade," he said.

"But the difference is that we live here, they don't. They're used to sitting around watching television in centrally heated apartments,' said Milo.

"I don't feel sorry for them. We didn't invite them to visit Ukraine. They invaded to steal from us and destroy our country.

We need to kick their asses back to Russia where they belong," said the NCO.

Milo felt more confident being back with his group and slept snuggly and warm in a farmhouse where three of his comrades were billeted with a lovely Ukrainian couple. The bedroom was warm and comfortable, and they each had a bed to themselves. A small fire crackled in the fireplace. They slept soundly but were all up at 0600 to wash, dress, and clean their rifles.

The farmer's wife cooked them a hearty breakfast and they all gave her some rubles and euros for her kindness. They also chopped some firewood and carried it in for them for their fire.

At 0800 they reunited with their NCO and went over plans for the days' mission.

A group of Russian soldiers with a tank had been terrorising a local village and was holding the mayor hostage. They had been going door to door, looting and plundering and unfortunately, raping some of the women. The mission was to destroy the tank and despatch the fifteen Russian soldiers who had been carrying out the atrocities.

"Do we take prisoners?" asked Milo.

"If we can, but due to their disgusting crimes, most of them have earned a bullet," said the NCO.

"Any other questions?" asked the NCO.

"How do we approach?" asked Freddie, the tall young fellow.

"First, we position our snipers around the rooftops and line up the tank with the bazooka to disable the tracks. Then when the tank's stationary, we fire from houses and we will catch them in an ambush," he explained, "All clear guys?"

They all nodded in agreement.

"What if something goes wrong?" asked Milo.

"As usual Milo, we disappear and meet back here at the rendezvous point,"

He told them, "Make every round count, aim, don't spray bullets," he said.

At the designated time the three snipers climbed up onto the roofs to assume their positions. A Ukrainian lady saw one of them climbing up and showed surprise, but when she noticed the yellow and blue insignia on his sleeves, she gave him the thumbs up and he pursed his lips to say, 'Sh!' She knew which side she was on.

Two Ukrainian soldiers came in through the back of the Inn and set up the Bazooka. At the edge of the street, they lined up the Stinger and armed a projectile.

Milo was with the foot soldiers armed with his AK-47 cocked and ready to fire.

As the Russian tank rumbled down the main street, the driver sat cockily in the turret with his fancy headgear and sunglasses, looking condescendingly upon the lesser mortals. Suddenly from the Inn door came a loud 'boom,' from the Bazooka. It disabled the right-hand track, bringing the tank to a sudden stop.

One of the snipers targeted the driver and hit him with an instantaneous head shot. His sunglasses went flying as he slumped forward, never to move again.

Other hatches opened but no-one climbed out. The Stinger was fired and scored a direct hit, blowing the tank to pieces. As previously mentioned, a dozen Russian soldiers came bustling out of the houses, alerted by the noise of the exploding tank, in turmoil without checking to see what had happened.

Five were shot down by rifle fire in the first instance while some of the others took cover and returned fire. This gradually proved ineffective as snipers with telescopic sights targeted them from above and picked them off one by one.

Milo accounted for three soldiers and winged a fourth. He showed no mercy for these rapists.

When the smoke of battle cleared, there was one wounded Russian soldier left alive. The acrid smell of burning flesh came from the flaming tank as those trapped inside had been unable to escape.

The wounded man lay writhing in pain and crying for his mother. Villagers came out of their houses and stood clapping and cheering.

Milo stemmed the flow of blood gushing from the wounded Russian's shoulder and shortly after the village doctor came out to assist him. He kicked away the soldier's weapon.

Milo's NCO yelled, "Grab any spare ammunition and weapons. We can use their stuff to kill them. Don't pity them. They invaded our country. Their people are sitting at home watching television, ours are being bombed."

The mayor was freed and thanked the squad for their bravery.

"You have saved my town and its people. How can we thank you?" asked Mayor Dimitri.

"We need some bread and some sausage if you can spare some please?" said the NCO.

He sent a villager off who soon returned with two big bags of supplies.

"Thank you, mayor. I'm sorry to leave you with this mess to clean up. Let us know if any more come here and we'll be back to get them," he reassured him, shaking hands.

The Ukrainian soldiers went off in different directions to walk back to the rendezvous point. That night they camped in the forest around a campfire. It was chilly but they soon huddled together and kept each other warm.

They had accounted for a tank and sixteen soldiers without losing any of their own fighters. The NCO said,

"We were lucky. Don't get cocky men, remain vigilant."

Grandfather Peter and Yuri loaded the scraped skins into the SUV.

"We should get quite a bit for these skins in Perm," said Grandfather Peter.

"Yes, it's a good bunch of hides. Have you got the list of supplies Elena wrote out for you?" asked Yuri.

"Yes Yuri, I have it in my coat pocket. I'll be back around 10.00 pm unless the snow falls heavier than this," he said.

Elana kissed him goodbye.

"Safe trip Grandfather," she called as he drove to the gate.

When he arrived in Perm he went straight to the tannery and received 180 euros for his load of high-quality hides.

"They're good quality Peter, not a mark on them," said the tanner.

"I think it's the weather. They grow thicker to keep out the cold," explained Peter.

"Do you think you could bag me a brown bear when you're out hunting?" he asked.

"I'll certainly try, but they tend to get mighty angry if you don't kill them with your first shot," said Peter, "I'll see what I can do."

Next, he drove to the general store to get their supplies and gave the shop assistant Elena's list.

"Yes, I can supply all these things Peter. Is your Elena still staying with you?" he asked.

"Yes, just the two of us, soon to be three. She's going to have a baby you know. That will make me a great grandfather."

"What became of her husband, a nice young fellow. He dropped in here once?" he asked.

"Didn't you know, he was conscripted into the army and sent to the war. He is missing, presumed dead, in Ukraine," lied Peter.

"Oh, I'm so sorry, I didn't know. That bloody war, who needs it!" he said.

With his supplies, Peter set off back to the cabin up in the mountains.

The snow began to fall heavily, and Peter found himself hurrying before he was literally snowed under. The bends were treacherous and to go off the road and over the side would mean almost certain death. But Peter had driven log trucks down the mountain trails here for a long time and at 9.30 pm he drove into the front gate to the cabin.

Yuri braved the conditions and came out to meet him.

"How did you go Peter?" he asked.

"Great, I got an excellent price for the skins, and I brought back all our supplies, but the bloody snow was terrible," he said.

Safely inside Peter warmed himself by the fire while Yuri and Elena unpacked the groceries. Yuri poured Grandfather Peter a vodka and he downed it to warm up inside.

"The man in the tannery wants us to bag him a brown mountain bear," said Peter.

"Have you ever killed one before?" asked Yuri.

"Yes, several, but it's not as easy as it sounds. Their skull is as if it's made out of metal and ordinary bullets seem to bounce off it and make it ferociously angry. To kill one, you have to strike it in the heart," said Peter.

"How much would you get for one?" asked Yuri.

"About five hundred euros or more," he replied.

"What do you think? I'm game if you are," said Peter.

"Let's do it," said Yuri, unafraid of an adventure.

"Don't mention it to Elena, she'll only try to talk us out of it," said Yuri.

Two days later Yuri and Peter strapped on their snowshoes, put on their heavy jackets, slung their rifles, and headed across the mountain to where Peter had noticed a brown bear fossicking for green moss on rocks under a snow ledge.

Although it was freezing in the stillness and their breath was coming out in smoky vapor, they both remained perfectly quiet and waited.

Eventually, along came a great brown bear, wallowing through the deep snow. Yuri got a sight on it at fifty metres and fired a perfect head shot at the big male bear.

Instead of dying, the bear reared up on its hind legs and came bounding at them at an alarming pace. Yuri fired several more shots that appeared to go astray as the bear was still coming so quickly.

When it reached them, it was upon them before they could move in their snowshoes. They were as if transfixed. The bear swiped at Yuri and knocked his rifle out of his hands sending him flying sideways. As the bear stood on its hind legs to swipe at Grandfather with its mighty claws, he fired a shot point blank into its chest. It slumped to the ground dead, pinning Yuri beneath it.

Yuri called out, "Help! Get me out of here before he eats me!"

Grandfather leaned down to him and said, "He can't eat you, Yuri. He's dead."

As Grandfather rolled the dead bear off him, it groaned a final exhalation of air and Yuri, thinking it was still alive, scurried out from underneath it.

Sometime later, he'd calmed down and Peter had the bear's skin off, ready to carry home. Yuri had a souvenir, a claw scrape across his right cheek, but was otherwise uninjured.

"He was going to kill me Peter," he said.

"That's okay Yuri, I had him covered," he answered.

"How long were you going to wait before you fired?" asked Yuri.

"I had to have a clear shot to hit him in the chest," he explained.

"That might have been just after he killed me," said Yuri.

"Better late than never. Regardless, I warned you that they have a very hard skull," he reminded.

They lugged the skin back on a pole.

"What about the bear meat?" asked Yuri.

"It won't be here, tomorrow, the wolves will have a feast tonight. Nature wastes nothing," he said.

When they arrived back at the cabin, Yuri was excited telling Elena what had happened.

"You fool. You could have got yourself killed. Who would be a father to our little baby? And look at your cheek. It's got a big claw mark on it," she scolded.

Grandfather smiled and said, "He's okay. We could always call him, 'Claude.'"

Elena frowned at this remark and cleaned the claw mark with antiseptic and covered it with a plaster and dressing.

"I don't think that you two have any common sense at all."

Outside in his shed, Grandfather stretched out the bear skin, scraped it and began the tanning process the next day.

"This should fetch us about five hundred euros, Yuri," Peter told him.

"Now we'll be able to afford some fuel," he said, smiling.

"We can now afford to buy a lot of things, 'Claude!'" he laughed.

Yuri felt his cheek and managed a proud grin.

After the attacking the tank in the village, Milo's Ukrainian battle unit moved on to seek out other Russian targets.

One of the highlights of the week was when a Ukrainian helicopter landed close by in a clearing and President Volodymir Zelensky climbed out. He strode over to Milo, the NCO, and the other soldiers in the unit and shook their hands and awarded medals for valour and commended them for their bravery.

He was a man, small in physical stature but full of charm and sincerity. He told the battle group that they would eventually win, and Ukraine would be free. He took time to speak with each soldier and ask where they were from.

He apologised for the brevity of his visit and that he would have to keep moving. It was only a short contact, but it gave the men such a boost in morale, but they supported and respected him and vowed to continue their efforts.

Amidst a whirlwind of swirling dust and grass, the helicopter lifted off and he was gone. At least, he visited them at the front line, where the real war was taking place and didn't hide at the end of long tables in huge palaces away from his people. This Zelensky, was a true leader.

Svetlana regained consciousness in the wreckage of the hospital and discovered immediately that she couldn't move her legs. There was still a lot of dust in the air and she found it difficult to breathe. She could hear sirens sounding from outside and voices shouting from various rescuers. Her head felt as if it was splitting in two.

She'd been going about her nursing duties on the third floor when the missile had slammed into the hospital in Kyiv. They'd had no warning, or time to run, or help anyone when the floor had completely collapsed. She vaguely recalled a deafening explosion and a falling sensation. As her senses cleared, she heard people shouting and digging away debris.

Finally, she managed to call out weakly,

"Help! Help! I can't move."

A short while later the face of a young soldier poked through a hole in the rubble.

"Don't worry, we'll soon have you out of here," he reassured her.

Another rescuer joined him and together they lifted the rubble that was pinning her legs.

"Can you wriggle your toes, Miss?" asked the young man.

"Yes, I don't think anything's broken," she answered.

They established that she'd been fortunate not to have any broken bones, but she had suffered multiple lacerations and scratches.

Together they eased her out from the debris carefully and at last she was free.

"What's your name?" asked the young soldier.

"Svetlana!" she answered with a smile.

"And yours?" she asked.

"Milo," he replied.

The other young man had left them to go off to continue searching for other survivors of the blast.

"How are we going to get out of here Milo?" she asked.

"I've got a long piece of string that I let out as we entered. We can follow it back the way I came in," he told her.

"That's clever. We'd be struggling if we had to find our way out, it all looks so different than it was," she commented.

But they'd spoken too soon and there was a subsequent collapse, and their exit was blocked by rubble. They huddled together and Milo shielded her from further falling debris.

"There was a stairwell over near that wall. Perhaps it's still intact. We could try and get out that way," she suggested.

She led the way and crawled ahead leading him to the stairwell.

"What about your comrade?" she asked.

Milo called his fellow rescuer on the radio he had attached to his utility belt and received a fuzzy reply.

"Are you okay Dimitri?" he called.

"I'm okay friend. I'm outside waiting for you guys," came the reply.

"I let him know that we're on our way out," he said.

When they reached the stairwell entrance it was blocked but Milo worked hard clearing debris and soon, they were poking their way down to the safety of the street below. It was very painful to walk and crawl. But after an hour, Milo had her in the back of an ambulance.

"You saved my life Milo. I am so grateful for you getting me out," she said sincerely, throwing her arms around him and kissing him.

"It's all in a days' work. It's just a shame that we had to meet under such difficult circumstances," he said to her.

The missile strike on a hospital, a war crime, had taken the lives of fifty people. Soldiers were still removing bodies from the destroyed hospital.

Svetlana wrote down Milo's details and passed hers on to him, vowing to catch up with him in Kyiv when they next had the opportunity.

Milo went back to his unit at the rendezvous and reported all that happened during his visit to Kyiv.

During many engagements Milo thought of Svetlana and wondered how she was getting on. Still the Russian missiles rained down on Ukraine. Would there ever be an end to this incredible madness. Meanwhile infrastructure was being destroyed and many lives, on both sides, were being lost.

Up in the Ural Mountains, Elena's pregnancy was progressing well. Grandfather and Yuri were providing food and warmth throughout the cold winter. When Yuri heard news of the war it saddened him. Many young Russian conscripts were losing their lives for very little gain. He realised the Ukrainians were fighting for their very existence and couldn't understand why President Putin had invaded their neighbouring country.

"Grandfather Peter, what do you think about it, this war against Ukraine?" asked Yuri.

"It's madness. All war is madness, and the common people do all the fighting and dying. The rich old men are safe in their palaces, eating their fine food while they send armies of young people to die. It has never been any different. Tolstoy's, 'War and Peace,' tells us this. I don't believe it will ever change," he said.

"That's easy Yuri. Anyone who makes weapons, bullets, tanks, missiles and fighter jets. They will make enormous profits out of all this. They always do," he answered.

Just then Elena came in with a tray with mugs of hot chocolate and biscuits and said,

"Stop making yourselves miserable talking about the war you two, have a hot mug of cocoa."

"She's right Yuri. There isn't much we can do about the war. Let's just stay out of it," Peter advised.

Milo was progressing towards a Russian battle group in a small village outside Bakhmut. The Russians were holed up inside a warehouse, fifteen of them. They were sitting around cleaning weapons when a Ukrainian tank fired upon them and practically wiped out the whole unit. Milo and his group went in to mop up. They found four soldiers still alive and they were in no mood for a firefight.

Quickly their wounds were dressed, and the NCO sent for a truck to collect them to join the prisoners that might be in turn used in the prisoner exchange program.

Milo gazed around at the contorted bodies of the Russian soldiers who had been killed in the attack. He felt physically sick and went to a corner to throw up. He knew they were invaders but the killing still affected him. The insanity of war was not lost on him.

The NCO asked, "Are you okay Milo?"

"I'll be alright. It's just all this killing. It makes me think it'll never end," he told him.

"When they stop sending their soldiers to Ukraine to kill our people, it will stop," said the NCO. They collected all the weapons and ammunition and left the bodies.

The Ukrainian battle group set off to their next mission.

That night Milo was sitting by the fire, looking into it when the NCO sat next to him.

"I think all this action is affecting you comrade Milo. It's very normal to become concerned about all the horrors of war. I want you to take a few weeks and go home for a break to recover. What do you think?" he asked.

"Only if I can be spared," he replied.

"You're one of our best men, but we need you well and ready," he answered.

A few days later Milo travelled to Kyiv. He looked up Svetlana, who was currently working at another hospital.

When he found her, she was serving meals to wounded patients and didn't notice him as he came into the ward. He watched her in action and saw how patient and kind she was by the way she spoke to her patients and fellow nurses.

"Milo!" she exclaimed when she saw him, "I didn't think I'd see you again. I'm almost finished my shift here. If you give me a hand, we can go back to my apartment and I'll cook us some dinner," pointing to a sink with a liquid soap dispenser.

"Collect and scrape the plates, then stack them into the dishwasher," she instructed.

Milo was a soldier, and he knew how to take orders. He scrubbed his hands and arms, donned some rubber gloves and began collecting plates and cutlery from patients who had completed their meals.

He glanced over at Svetlana who was dressed in a white nurse's smock tied at the back and her long auburn hair was up in a bun. She smiled at him when she saw him watching her. She was the very picture of grace and loveliness. He was dressed in his camouflage fatigues with his short hair slicked back.

When they'd completed the duty, the night shift came on and they were free to leave.

Milo noticed that she still had a few scratches and bruises from the previous ordeal but seemed to be walking freely. She held his hand with fingers locked and as they passed a shop window they stopped, and she kissed him.

"I never did thank you for saving me Milo," she whispered, and he felt wonderful.

There were several cars and army vehicles driving past them in the street and one young soldier poked his head out and 'wolf-whistled,' when he saw Svetlana. She just smiled and waved back to him.

"He's a cheeky fellow," she commented, "but he's fighting for our freedom too, just like you."

They soon arrived at her apartment building on Dart Street and climbed the three flights of stairs up to her unit. They were almost bowled over by her pet cat, 'Bushy,' who came around her for a pat and some food.

Svetlana fed him from a can in the refrigerator and told Milo to take off his boots and relax while she got dinner underway. The apartment was small but neat and she had uniforms and underwear on the airing horse.

"May I help you with dinner?" he offered.

"No Milo, tonight is your treat. Sit down, turn on the television, and relax for once. You must be very tired from all the fighting," she remarked.

"No, I'm fine really. I could set the table, or peel some vegetables for you," he offered.

"You're a darling. Alright, here are four potatoes for you to peel," she said, handing him the knife.

As he washed and peeled the potatoes, he had a feeling of peace and normalcy that he thought had disappeared completely from his life.

Svetlana cooked a lovely stew, and he passed her the cut potatoes which she put into it. As she stood stirring and cooking the food, Milo held her gently from behind and softly kissed her lovely smooth neck. He could discern the natural scent of her freshly washed hair and the warmth of her body. He thought he was in Heaven.

"Later," she scolded, "we don't want to spoil the stew.'

She wheeled around and she let him taste a sample of the stew from a large wooden spoon.

"Yum!" he said, "It tastes great!"

Then she kissed him.

"You taste great too, my handsome soldier," she cooed.

She dished up the meal for each of them and lit a candle on the table. They sat down, opposite each other and she bowed her head and said grace.

"Lord, please end this terrible war and take away all the suffering of those involved. Grant us peace."

"Amen!" said Milo, not knowing what else to say.

As they were enjoying their first meal together, they got to know each other better and spoke about their lives before the war had broken out. Milo told her about his job as a computer technician and of how he had studied at Kyiv University.

Svetlana told him that this was her first year as a nurse and that she had attended Kyiv University too, but she had never met him there.

"It's funny how it took a disaster to bring us to know each other," she said.

She brought out a bottle of chilled wine from the refrigerator and poured them both a glass.

Milo made a toast, "To peace!" he said.

They clinked their glasses and drank. During their discussion Milo related the experience he had encountered with Yuri and of how they had become friends.

Svetlana hung on his every word and wondered what made this exciting man tick.

He was drawn deeply into her, amazed by the absolute beauty of her grey-blue eyes. When they'd finished at the table, they adjourned to the big comfortable lounge and continued their conversation.

After a while Svetlana put her finger up to his lips to silence him. She melted into his arms and kissed him with unbridled passion. All their sadness and horror washed away as they loved one another. Milo had never felt such complete passion and happiness. Sure, he had been with other girlfriends at university, but this was very different.

Before long they made their way to the bedroom, consummating their beautiful relationship. They spent hours together, loving, talking softly and simply enjoying each other.

"Does this mean we're going steady?" he asked, playfully,

"Going steady! We'd better be, you weren't wearing protection," she replied.

'What did you want me to wear, my helmet?" he responded.

"Is there anyone else Milo. You're not married, are you?" she asked seriously.

"No! No wife. No other girlfriends! No fiance," he said.

"Well, that's okay. I'm single too. But now it's just you and me, okay?" she asked.

"Yes! You and me!" he answered.

"I'm worried about you getting hurt in the war Milo," she said.

"Me too," said Milo, "But having you gives me a reason to stay alive now. I have a reason to go on living. But it's not even safe in Kyiv. Remember how I met you in that bombed out hospital. Today, nowhere is safe. We could try to get out to Finland, or somewhere else safer," he told her.

"I think we're both too patriotic to leave Ukraine while we're needed here Milo," she said.

"I suppose you're right, but I want a good life with you, a home, kids, a job and vacations. I don't want this war. Damn Putin!" he said strongly.

As they spoke the air raid sirens began to wail, signalling the beginning of yet another drone or missile attack.

"Here we go again!" shouted Svetlana.

"Where do we go?" asked Milo.

"Down to the subway, quickly, get some warm clothes on but leave everything else. We have about three minutes before they start bombing us," she warned.

He responded and they dressed quickly.

"Bring your coat, you'll need it down there," she advised.

They wasted no time in getting down to the subway and sat on a blanket she'd grabbed and brought down for them. They huddled closely together as the drones and missiles crashed indiscriminately into surrounding buildings above them. They could hear the deafening explosions, and dust fell in upon everyone causing coughing and discomfit.

As they clung together in the subway Milo was heard to say,

"How did it come to this? Less than a year ago we were getting on with our lives, working for our future, then everything changed with this invasion."

"Hopefully our army can repel them and send them back over the border to their own country, and we can get back on with our lives," she replied.

A little boy of about seven years of age came up to Milo in the dark and spoke,

"Mister I'm scared. Are we going to die?"

Milo put his arm around him and told him,

"We'll be alright. Soon the 'all clear' will sound and we'll be able to go home. You'll see. Where's your mother?"

"She's over against the wall crying, near the steps," he said.

"She's upset. We're all a little upset, but we're safe down here and it'll be over soon. Go back to your mother now or she'll be even more upset," said Milo.

The boy went back to his mother.

"It's hard on everyone, especially the little kids," said Svetlana.

"Are you alright?" asked Milo.

"I'm okay. But I'm glad that I have you here beside me," she answered.

There were lots of people sheltering in the subway and there were still occasional explosions coming from above. Every time they heard one, Svetlana cuddled against him, and they both sat still and waited.

After two hours the attack ended and fifteen minutes later, the 'all-clear' siren sounded out. People began to file up the stairs with their bags and possessions to head for home.

Nobody knew what they'd be going back to find.

Perhaps their homes had been destroyed, perhaps they remained still standing. Milo and Svetlana were lucky. Her apartment was just as they'd left it. Her neighbour's apartment two doors up had been completely destroyed. Fortunately, the residents had taken shelter in the subway.

Milo and Svetlana made hay while sun shone and spent almost all their time together, loving, dining out and just plain enjoying being together. Over a glass of wine in their favourite restaurant Milo suggested that they move to Finland.

"There's no peace here," said Milo, "this bloody war is set to go for years. At least if we get to Helsinki we could decide where we'd like to live, get a home and have a family. What do you think Lana?"

"It would mean leaving our home to the invaders," she said.

"We can't kill them all, even with NATO's help, there are too many Russians for us to beat off," he said.

"So, you want to give up and let them have 'our' country," she replied.

"No matter how hard we fight or how many sacrifices we make this is a war that we can never win. No matter what Zelensky says," he said.

"With that attitude we'll never win," she said sternly.

"But can't you see that this is one of our last chances to get away and begin a new life in Finland. At least five million people have migrated.

"If that's how you feel, then go. I will stay in Kyiv and do my duty until I am no longer able to do it," she said.

"I thought you loved me, Lana?" he said.

"I do, I do love you. But I can't leave my country and my people, people who need me, to live in a safe, comfortable life while my country burns," she said.

"You're impossible Lana. But if that's how you feel, I will stay too!" he said.

She kissed him and smiled and said,

"I knew you would say that. My hero!"

"In any case, I have to leave Kyiv tomorrow and go back to my battle group. My leave has expired," he told her.

They spent one last night of love together and were up early making breakfast and packing his kitbag. Jokingly he asked,

"Have you seen my AK-47, I had it when I arrived?" he asked.

"It's in the closet. I don't like guns," she told him.

"They do come in handy during a firefight," he told her.

"When will I see you again Milo?" she asked.

"I don't know. I'll try and get back here on leave in about six weeks if they allow me to," he told her.

"Milo and Svetlana embraced warmly and finally he had to turn and leave to return to his comrades in the barracks outside Kyiv. He got to the rendezvous with his transport and was soon travelling back to Donetsk and the front. He travelled most of the day and renewed friendships with his fellow soldiers.

The preceding two weeks seemed a blur. He missed Svetlana already and the peace of their life together in Kyiv. He wished that his two weeks leave was beginning all over again.

But now his mind went back to the war, the indefinite struggle, the gloom and tragedy, the death and destruction. He heard the sounds of war long before his army truck arrived in the region. The air was punctuated by the explosion of artillery shells exploding. Two weeks is a long time in war and the fortunes of war ebb and flow, so it was in Soledar, the salt producing town.

Milo slotted back into his unit as if he had never been away. His comrades were glad to see him and welcomed him back with open arms. He was ordered directly back to the battle and found himself facing up to a Russian tank which had taken out complete positions of Ukrainian soldiers. He aimed a Stinger missile and fired from the shoulder. The tank exploded into fire in a spectacular explosion, the unprepared crew were killed instantly. A mighty unanimous cheer erupted from the surrounding defenders.

Immediately the Ukrainian soldiers jumped out from their cover and charged forward once more raking the Russian positions with machine gun and rifle fire. An occasional hand grenade flew towards a fortified farmhouse. The Russians turned and ran for their lives.

Many fell where they stood. There were many wounded from both sides lying in the mud screaming in pain.

Milo was sick of this terrible scene. What was it all for? These young men, being killed, were barely twenty years old. The furious battle raged on, and hours passed. Only darkness brought some respite and medics attempted to provide assistance to the fallen.

"Fall back to the farmhouse!" ordered the NCO.

Milo obeyed and lugged his missile projector on his shoulder. In the shelter of a wall, he reloaded his magazine with ammunition and collected and armed a new Stinger missile to fire.

"Get some hot food and rest up. You've earned it comrades," yelled the NCO. I think they've had enough for today."

Milo leaned his aching back against the wall. He wondered about Svetlana.

"Perhaps she's feeding the sick and wounded in the hospital," he thought to himself.

This war was never ending. This place was smashed, burnt-out and destroyed. Even if the Russians took this godforsaken town, what good would it do them. All it had to offer was, salt. Milo was overcome with battle fatigue and the hopelessness of the situation.

Up in the Ural Mountains, Elena was growing bigger every day and was rapidly approaching full term. The weather was even colder and the temperature dropped to -40 degrees. Yuri considered a trip to the warmth and safety of Finland. If they could get across the border, Elena could give birth in a real hospital, perhaps in Helsinki.

"What do you think Grandfather Peter. Can we make it?" he asked.

"Who knows. This world has gone crazy. No-one knows where the border guards are stopping people from leaving Russia," he answered.

"You might be lucky," answered Peter.

"But you're safe here for the time being. But I can understand how you're getting nervous about the birth of your baby," said Grandfather.

The quietness of the cabin was shattered by the ringing of Elena's mobile phone summoning them loudly. Yuri answered it and was surprised to find that it was Milo on the line. "How are you comrade. Are you safe?" asked Yuri.

"I'm on active duty outside Soledar. We're under heavy attack by the Russians. I don't think I'm going to get out of here alive, my friend. Has your baby been born yet?" asked Milo.

"No baby yet. But it's so cold here in the mountains that I wouldn't want to come out either," said Yuri.

Milo laughed.

"I've met and fallen in love with a nurse I found trapped in Kyiv, in a bombed out hospital. I've tried to convince her to get out and go to Finland, but she insists on staying and doing her duty for the country. Do you think you'll leave the Urals and head to Finland?" he asked.

"If we can make it through the border crossings that's what we'd like to do. Then Elena can have the baby in a real hospital," explained Yuri.

"If I can persuade Svetlana to leave, we'll be leaving as well. She's convinced that we'd be deserting our duty. If we get there, I'll catch up with you," said Milo.

The phone reception became garbled, and they were disconnected.

"What was that all about?" asked Elena.

"It was my Ukrainian friend, Milo. He has fallen in love with a nurse, and he is trying to convince her to leave Ukraine and flee to Finland, but he can't persuade her to leave. She wants to stay and administer aid to the unfortunate victims of the war," he told her.

"She sounds very noble. I don't think he'll have much success persuading her to leave with him, do you?" she asked.

"I don't know. It also depends on how much she loves him and wants to be with him. Surely, she can see that she's trapped in a hopeless situation," she added.

"We've got to think about our own lives and our future, not only for us, but also for our child," he told her.

Yuri and Elena began preparations for their journey to Finland timed to coincide with the Spring thaw.

Yuri prepared documents to fool the border guards under the pseudonym of 'Alexander Kasynski'. They wouldn't be interested in Elena. He would tell them he was taking her to her mother's home for the birth of their child.

Yuri ran the idea by Grandfather Peter, and he thought it would probably be the best plan they could come up with. In preparation for the long journey, Peter drove to Perm and filled the SUV with fuel as well as two jerrycans.

"Have you calculated the distance you have to travel Yuri?" Elena, enquired.

"I think our best route is from Perm to Kouvola in Finland. It should take about twenty-eight hours if we have no hold ups and the road is clear,' he told her.

He pulled out Peter's map.

"We'll drive to Perm, then north-west to Dvina, then north again to Arkangelisk, around the White Sea coast to the Finland border. If we get across, when we get across, we'll drive to Kouvola. It's a two-hour drive from Kouvola to Helsinki. We'll apply for asylum there and seek out a hospital for you to have the baby," he said, "Well that's the plan."

"We'll have to take plenty of food and drink as we'll be on the road for at least a couple of days," she chimed in.

"Are you afraid?" he asked.

"No. I was afraid when you went away in the war. I thought you were going to get killed and leave me a widow with a child," she answered.

"No, you're going to be a wife with a husband and a child," he said.

They were leaving on a Friday so on Thursday night they had a farewell dinner together in front of the fire. There was a sadness upon them as they realised that they wouldn't be seeing Peter for a long time. Yuri promised to send him a photo of the baby when it arrived. Grandfather Peter would be sad to see them go but realised that they were making a decision for their future together.

Still, he'd enjoyed having Yuri and Elena stay with him and going hunting together. He was also going to miss Elena's cooking. She had made a big difference to the usual diet on which he'd been subsisting.

They all hugged and said their farewells, then were off on yet another venture.

They were heading into the unknown.

The SUV made good time as they travelled towards Perm. They arrived there a few hours later and then turned north-west towards

Dvina. They chatted happily as they drove along the roads that had snow along the sides. Yuri, drove carefully, realising that a skid would only delay them.

They came at last to a little roadside petrol station for a comfort stop and Yuri topped up the fuel. Elena poured him a hot coffee from a thermos flask she had prepared prior to their departure. She'd also baked some cookies and dunked one in the coffee and savoured it.

They were soon back on the road again travelling ever north-west towards Dvina. It began to turn dark, so Yuri turned on his headlights and driving lights. Fortunately, no animals jumped out on the road in front of them. They reached Dvina but continued driving to Arkangelisk.

Yuri was becoming very weary but realised that they'd have to keep driving. When they reached the highway to Arkangelisk, Elena squeezed in behind the wheel and drove to give Yuri a break. She'd managed a snooze earlier, so she was fresh.

The highway was smooth, and it was good clear driving weather apart from a few occasional patches of fog. At last, when Yuri awoke, he felt much better, and pulled over for some coffee and a stretch. Being pregnant, Elena had a sore back, so Yuri massaged it for her.

Feeling refreshed, they drove on and reached Arkangelisk as the morning sun was rising. It wouldn't be long now until they'd be driving around the White Sea coast and out of Russia.

This, of course, would involve crossing the border and all the associated complications of border guards.

"This is it!" he thought,

Driving around the coastline was scenic and was a pleasant contrast to the snow-covered Ural Mountains from where they'd come and the safety of Grandfather Peter's comfortable cabin.

When Yuri and Elena finally arrived at the Russian-Finland border they found their way blocked by heavily armed guards.

There was simply no way through. As they watched, from a safe vantage point up the hill, they saw a number of vehicles ordered to turn around and head back the way they'd come. They weren't letting anyone through. Some unfortunate individuals were dragged out of their cars, bludgeoned with rifle butts and thrown into a collection military vehicle.

Yuri considered their situation and was convinced their position was hopeless.

Just then, he heard a voice coming from the bushes beside the vehicle.

"Pst! It's me Ivan, for a price, I can show you a mountain road around the road- block," he whispered loudly.

"I'm interested comrade Ivan. Tell me, how much do I need to pay you for this help?" asked Yuri.

"Are ten thousand rubles too much?" asked Ivan.

"I haven't got that much. But I have five thousand rubles and three quality reindeer hides and an AK-47 I can throw in if you like," bargained Yuri.

"Okay comrade. It's a deal! Do you mind if I drive?" requested Ivan.

"Sure, you know this area better than me," he said.

Ivan climbed into the driver's seat and performed a tricky U-turn on the narrow mountain road. Soon they found themselves travelling down the mountain.

They reached a farm gate and Yuri got out and opened it. Ivan drove through and Yuri got back in when he'd closed the gate.

They drove for what seemed like ages until they came to a high ridge that looked quite treacherous. Yuri was glad he'd let Ivan take the wheel as he appeared familiar with the track.

As the sun set, they reached the Finnish border and drove across it without incident.

"This is where I leave you comrade. You are now safely in Finland. I suggest you camp here tonight and at first light tomorrow continue along this road which will lead you eventually to Helsinki," he announced.

"But how are you going to get back Ivan?" he asked.

"Do you see that cabin over there on the hill, that's my house. I'll hitch a ride back down to the border crossing and guide another group over tomorrow. That's how I make a living comrade. I'll soon be a rich man," he said.

"By the way," said Yuri, "Thank you for helping us and here is your payment."

He handed Ivan five thousand rubles, the three fine hides and the AK-47 as he'd no longer be needing it. Ivan thanked him, shook hands and waved to Elena.

"Good luck with your baby," he called as he turned and walked away lugging his reindeer hides.

Yuri lit a fire and cooked their evening meal. It was a chilly night but the hot food warmed them and the glorious star-filled heavens put on a mighty light show for them. They felt as if they were on top of the world. They were free, and they were together.

When Yuri and Elena reached Helsinki, they went directly to the Red Cross building and sought assistance registering as asylum seekers. They answered honestly and Yuri told them he was a conscientious objector. They were very lucky to be accepted as free immigrants. Next, they looked for a hospital to assist with the impending birth of their baby.

Once again, they were fortunate to find the assistance they needed. The Red Cross found them accommodation in a well-appointed apartment in the suburbs of the city. People were nervous about the war, but life seemed quite normal. Television newscasts presented footage of the war in Ukraine. They felt sad when they saw young soldiers like Yuri being killed and injured in the wretched war.

Sometimes Elena cried and lamented the terrible situation on the screen, night after night.

"When's it all going to end Yuri? Now the English, the Americans and the Germans are sending their Leopard tanks for the war. Even more young Russian men are going to be killed," she said.

"President Putin might be deposed from power and peace will once more be upon us," said Yuri.

Milo charged to a forward position as the Wagner forces were mown down.

The Ukrainian heavy machine guns fired unrelenting deadly bursts of bullets and the mortars landed on the outskirts of Bakhmut. It was a bloody slaughter. It had been described as a 'meat grinder.' Only the meat in this was human beings.

"These Wagner mercenaries must be on drugs. They don't go down straight away. They have to bleed out before they stop charging," said the NCO.

"Yes, I reckon you're right," said Milo, "do you think we can beat them off Boss?"

"I don't know, we can only try," he replied.

As he spoke Milo felt a searing pain as a bullet slammed into his shoulder sending him reeling around backwards, his machine gun flying from his hands.

Two medics ran to assist him and staunched the bleeding, holding wadding over his wound. His legs went weak from loss of blood, so they carried him on a stretcher back to the aid station. He blacked out due to the intense pain and loss of blood.

When he regained consciousness, he was in the back of a field ambulance headed towards Kyiv. Svetlana was shocked when she saw him being carried into the emergency department. Her heart sank when she realised that he could die from his wound and the blood loss.

The doctor wasted no time in transfusing blood into him. His blood type was stamped onto his dog tag, which expedited the process."

Milo's eyes sprang open, and he couldn't believe what he was seeing. There, bending over him was Svetlana, dressed in her scrubs attending to his shoulder wound. There were tears running down her cheeks.

"Oh Milo, when I told you that we needed to stay and fight for our country, I didn't mean you had to go out and die for it," she said.

"I was fighting for us, and our country" he said.

"Would you still like to go to Finland Milo? Now I can see that life is too dangerous for us here," she told him.

"I spoke to my friend Yuri and his wife Elena on the cell phone, and he told me that he and his wife were heading out of Russia to Finland. We could do something similar and meet up with them. Our lives could be much better for all of us. We could come back to Ukraine when the war is over," said Milo.

"That's if it's ever going to be over," he added.

He was heavily sedated, and his transfusion was still taking place.

"Are you in pain Milo?" she asked.

"Apart from this great hole in my shoulder, I'm feeling wonderful," he said, tripping out on pain medication.

It took him almost a week before he could sit up and move his arm again.

He saw lots of young soldiers being brought in to be treated for their wounds.

Having Svetlana around to console him and speak to, assisted his recovery. He was amazed at her skill and resilience as she went about her nursing tasks. He was moved to a ward where he could receive rehabilitation exercises as well as wound care. He was shocked by the serious nature of the casualties being brought in regularly. After seeing them, he considered himself fortunate that his wound was not as drastic as some of theirs.

One poor fellow was brought in with his legs completely missing because he had stepped on a land mine. He witnessed first-hand the valuable work all the doctors and nurses were performing day in and day out.

Svetlana came to him to perform his observations and dress his wound.

"Good. It's looking better already but you're going to have a nice souvenir of the war," she kidded.

"Would you like to leave with me and travel to Finland? We can get married there," he proposed.

"Oh Milo, I'd love to come and become your wife," she said.

She leaned forward and kissed him.

Just as she did so, the Director of Nursing happened to come by and said,

"Well, that's one way of helping our young patients to get better. Do you treat all our patients the same way Sister Svetlana?" she added sarcastically.

"He's a VIP Matron," she smiled, "This man is going to be my husband."

When Milo recovered, they made plans to travel to Finland to meet up with Yuri and Elena.

Milo and Svetlana had a much easier journey into Finland than their friends and were fortunate to be included on a medivac flight from Kyiv to Helsinki. When they passed through customs, they attempted to phone Yuri and Elena. This proved harder than it had first appeared, but a week later, after an interview with the Red Cross officials, the two couples reunited.

Yuri and Elena were in the lovely apartment that they had been allocated when Milo knocked on their door, Yuri's eyes could not believe what they saw.

"Milo! It's you! How did you find us?" he exclaimed.

He hugged Milo and kissed him on both cheeks. Then he turned to Svetlana and said,

"Who is this beautiful lady?"

"I present my fiancé, Svetlana," announced Milo.

"And please meet my lovely wife, Elena!" said Yuri.

"You're a lucky man Yuri," said Milo.

"Please sit down. We're so glad to see you both,' said Elena.

"Milo has told me all about you Yuri. This terrible war had brought us to this place in our lives," said Svetlana.

Over a bottle of fine wine and a meal the four of them sat relating their experiences since they had last met.

"The trip over the border was a real adventure," said Elena, as they sat spellbound listening. Yuri's story about the bear hunt caught their attention as he described being attacked. They all laughed when he told them that Grandfather Peter had nicknamed him 'Claude,' after the incident.

"Never shoot a brown bear in the head," advised Yuri, "The bullets just bounce off."

Milo told them about how he'd been wounded and took off his shirt and showed them his scar to prove it.

"You're very lucky to have survived Milo," said Elena.

"I wouldn't have survived had it not been for Svetlana and the skilful medical team. I saved her life and then she saved mine," he said.

Svetlana laughed at this, and her laughter was fresh and delightful to hear.

Their apartment was centrally heated and comfortable and soon they were all feeling tired and ready for bed.

"I'll pull out the convertible sofa and you can sleep in here if you like?" said Yuri.

"That would be nice," said Svetlana.

"In the morning we can look for an apartment, if you decide to stay here, said Yuri.

Later that night, as they were cuddled up in bed together, they discussed their future.

"Milo!" she said, out of the blue, "We really should go back to Ukraine and help our people. How can we live here safely in Finland, while they die for our freedom and the future of our country?"

"I thought that you'd decided to get out while we still could so that we can do what 'we' want to do, have children, a home and a future," said Milo.

"You can stay if you want to and I will go back and serve my people and save their lives,' she told him.

Milo thought about what she was saying and eventually came to a similar conclusion.

"Of course, you are right Lana. I am a soldier. I can fight the invaders and protect our people. We must go back. I understand Yuri and Elana, they are escaping from a terrible place and almost certain death. Their President wants to use them as cannon fodder. He doesn't care if his soldiers die or not."

The next morning, they spoke with their friends about what they had discussed. Of course, Yuri and Elena tried to dissuade them. They didn't want them to go back to war torn Ukraine. But they soon realised that Svetlana and Milo were determined to go back and serve their country and they would support them.

"Well at least you two might consider 'tying the knot,' while you're here. At least we can attend your wedding," said Yuri.

'How about it, Lana? Would you consider it? Will you marry me?" asked Milo.

"Why not," she replied, "We can get married here in Helsinki and then go home as husband and wife," she said.

Yuri and Elena helped with the arrangements at the Russian Orthodox church and Father Dimitri Francis agreed to preside over the ceremony. They would hold their reception at 'Pompier,' a prestigious French restaurant.

It was a small affair but the love and sincerity emanating from them made it all that more enjoyable.

Elena served as Svetlana's matron of honour and Yuri served as Milo's best man. For a short juncture, the war disappeared, and all was celebration.

After a week of love and absolute happiness, Milo and his gorgeous bride boarded the flight to fly back to Ukraine. Yuri and Elena saw them off but wondered if they'd ever see them again.

They arrived back safely and were almost swallowed up immediately by duties. Milo reported to his battle group and Svetlana reported to the hospital to resume assisting the wounded with their medications.

Yuri and Elana, on the other hand, reported to the Helsinki Hospital where their little baby boy, 'Peter,' was born on a cold, wet afternoon. Yuri supported her throughout the birth and fortunately there were no complications.

Yuri gazed into his baby's eyes and wondered what life had in store for him. Whatever it was, Yuri wished him peace and happiness.

They were so happy to have their little baby and Yuri cuddled them both.

The Russian President walked from the Kremlin to his waiting black limousine. As he was about to climb into the back seat two bullets struck him.

One slammed into his head, and the other hit him in the midsection. He dropped to the ground instantly and lay there twitching and bleeding. One of his generals rushed over to him and knelt beside him to hear him speak.

He rasped, "Nuke the US!" in a gurgling voice, then died.

Another general came over to them with two armed soldiers,

"What did he say comrade?" they asked.

"Patriotic to the end, he said, 'Long live Russia!'" lied the general.

In his prison cell Navalny was visited by his lawyer, Rudi Bandoff, who announced, "It's over, Putin is dead!"

Navalny's disposition altered, and he smiled.

"You are free to leave! They won't prevent you from leaving now my friend," said Bandoff.

Navalny began to pack his belongings and documents.

Then, with a start, Yuri awoke from his deep slumber, it had been just a dream. Putin hadn't been assassinated. He was still alive, and Navalny was still in a prison cell. The war was continuing as usual.

When he visited Elena and little Peter in the hospital, he mentioned the dream and she told him,

"It's only wishful thinking my love, he's too well protected. He realises that he has many enemies who would love to see him eliminated. That's why he hides behind big, long tables all the time," she said.

Milo looked out over the apparently empty field and scanned the surroundings his with infrared binoculars. He kept searching, refusing to believe that the field was empty.

"Reconnaissance messaged us and advised that four T-72B1 tanks had been sighted by a drone and were heading into this sector. They can't simply disappear," he said to a new recruit, Alexei, who had been assigned to him.

After a few more minutes searching, he exclaimed,

"They are in that Grove of trees."

"I can't see them Milo," he said.

"The infrared binoculars don't lie comrade," he answered, "They can't hide from them."

"What shall we do? to take on four is a big challenge, even for our brave unit," he asked.

"I'll call in an air strike from the Ukrainian Airforce. Our boys should be able to deal with them if I relay the co-ordinates," advised Milo.

He communicated over the field radio and gave the squadron the exact position co-ordinates of the Russian tanks and received confirmation that the air strike would take place in fifteen minutes.

Milo, Alexei and the other Ukrainian soldiers they alerted took cover and waited.

Right on time they heard the roar of the Ukrainian jets streaking towards their targets. When they were within range the heat seeking missiles locked on and hit home with devastating results. The four tanks were blown to pieces in a gigantic explosion of force. The tank crews had no chance of escaping and were consumed in the fireballs that engulfed them.

From their position of safety, the soldiers felt the heat from the explosions but shielded their eyes and were unharmed. This was Alexei's first experience of battle, and he was quite shocked by the firepower displayed.

When it was safe to do so, they inspected the damage and took photos to report back to HQ.

Alexei saw the burnt bodies of the tank crews and was horrified.

"Doesn't it affect you Milo, seeing all this death and destruction?"

"Every time. I wish no-one had to die. I wish there was no war. But while they keep sending soldiers and tanks to kill us, what alternative do we have?"

"It's just so sad, seeing all these young men being killed," said Alexei.

"It is very sad, but we didn't start this. But now we're obliged to finish it," said Milo.

After they'd taken any remaining weapons and ammunition Milo's battle unit retreated to the rendezvous point and reported to HQ.

"Well done!" said the CO, "That's four tanks that won't be wreaking havoc."

Svetlana went about her nursing duties providing care for the sick and wounded but she was consoled by the fact that she was married to a handsome hero, Milo. She smiled more readily and there was a friendlier edge in her voice as she dressed wounds and cared for her patients. She generated hope and inspired her patients to get better.

One night when she was finished her duties at the hospital, she received a phone call from Milo.

"Oh Milo! It's so good to hear your voice. How are things at the front in Bakhmut?" she asked.

"We are fighting hard, but they keep sending more tanks and soldiers," he told her.

"I miss you, Milo. I am busy here. I am very busy looking after wounded soldiers. They keep coming, Ukrainian and Russians. We treat them all, after all they are all human beings, just like us," she told him.

"Have you heard from Yuri and Elena?" he asked.

"Yes, they're enjoying their little baby they called 'Peter,'" she said.

"We could have a baby too," said Milo.

"Do you think it would be a good idea bringing a child into this world during this terrible war?" she asked.

"Yuri and Elena did, didn't they," he said.

"When can you come and see me, Milo? When can you get leave?" she said.

"I'm not due for leave, I've just returned to duty," he told her.

She began to cry, her heart breaking to be with him.

"I have to go now, Lana, the NCO is signalling for me to hang up," said Milo.

"I love you," she said.

"I love you too Darling," he said hanging up.

"Where is Yuri?" said the big KGB operative, "We know he was staying here. He's on our wanted list for crimes against our nation. We have to apprehend and make an example of him. Now, where is he?"

Peter was bleeding from the lip where they had punched him during interrogation.

"If I did know where he was I wouldn't tell you anyway," said Peter, defiantly.

For this reply he received another heavy blow to the head that sent him spinning sideways out of the chair and onto the cabin floor.

He was tied at the arms and the feet. He lay on the floor, his head spinning, wondering if they were going to kill him. They raided his cupboard and began drinking his vodka until they both passed out on the lounge chairs by the fire.

Peter wriggled out of his bonds and made his way stealthily to his milking shed. He picked up his hunting rifle and loaded cartridges into the magazine. They hadn't anticipated what was coming when he returned to the cabin and shot them both. He dragged out their lifeless bodies and left them for the nocturnal visitors, the hungry wolves. Peter had fought the Nazis and had been questioned by the Gestapo. He'd been lucky to have survived then, and these Gestapo-like KGB thugs were no better.

He dressed his injuries and settled down to a hot meal, not caring about the feast going on outside. The following day he disposed of the KGB operatives' car in a nearby river along with their weapons.

"They won't be bothering us again," he thought to himself.

"Milo, HQ is the line," said the communication officer, "They want to speak with you."

Milo came to the phone. They'd never called him before, and he was suspicious as to why they'd want to talk to him now.

"Hello Corporal Milosovic, my name is Major Pushenko. I've reviewed your service record and I congratulate you. The reason for this call is that I would like you to join our training squad to be sent to Germany to man the new Leopard II tank training group. They have been donated to Ukrainian military to repel the Russian forces as they are preparing their Spring offensive.

It will mean leaving your current battle group in Bakhmut, flying to Berlin and participating in the training program," he said.

"I will serve my country in any way I can Sir. I am pleased to accept your offer," answered Milo.

"I thought you would. It beats footslogging in the mud and snow, and every tank is heated. Report to the helicopter pad rendezvous at the co-ordinates I've sent you and you'll be flying out on Friday at 0700. Ukraine needs you," he advised, hanging up.

Milo began to pack his kit and unloaded his weapons, making them ready to travel. When he told Alexei what had transpired the young fellow was sad.

"Who's going to guide me through the action?" he asked.

"You're a good soldier now Alexei. Support your comrades and you'll get through it okay," he encouraged.

The noisy chopper landed on the helipad and Milo threw in his kit and climbed into a seat. His NCO waved him off.

He yelled, "Go and get 'em Milo!"

With that the clattering helicopter took off and headed west up over the trees.

It landed at an air force base where Milo transferred to a transport aircraft for the three hour flight to Berlin.

As they descended over the bustling German capital, Milo realised that life was continuing, completely oblivious to the terrible war going on in Ukraine.

The airport was a hive of activity with planes landing and taking off with alarming regularity. There were approximately twenty-eight soldiers in Milo's training squad, each with their blue and yellow shoulder flashes. They were all very fit young men and women and seemed to be in good spirits as they progressed towards their adventure crewing modern Leopard II tanks,

First, they were shown to their accommodation at the army base outside Berlin and assembled in the mess hall for a meal. The facilities were modern and spacious and the food that was served up was excellent quality compared to the field rations on which they'd been subsisting.

Milo was introduced to Ilya, a fellow trainee and they soon became close friends. The following morning, they were on parade at 0600 where the training officer divided them into tank crews. They were issued with new uniforms and berets. They were all given side arms and utility belts.

Milo's crew consisted of himself, as Commander, Ilya as Gunner, Vincent as Loader and Vasily as Driver. They were marched to a briefing room where the instructors showed them images of the latest Leopard II tank.

"The Bunderswehr has upgraded the Leopard II tank to become the most modern, powerful and effective fighting machine in the world today. But always remember, it will only ever be as effective as its crew.

It has 450 mm rolled homogenous armour that allows a durable battle readiness and has armaments that, can penerate the frontal armour of a Soviet tank at 2000 metres and a T-62 at 4000 metres. It has two 7.62 mm machine guns and is powered by a turbo charged diesel engine capable of 1500 horsepower. It boasts digital sighting, upgraded communications and is arguably the best tank available in our time.

After a Q and A session the trainees were shown to a huge green shed. Around the sides were tank simulators with large computer screens in front of them.

Each simulator had two instructors dressed in orange overalls to train the crews in the operation techniques. Milo's crew sat in their positions digitally sighting, loading and firing simulated rounds into targets that appeared with scheduled rapidity on the monitor before them, something akin to a very sophisticated parlour computer game.

At first the crews were firing wide or over the top of the targets and were being hit by incoming rounds, but gradually their accuracy began to improve. By the end of the first session the Ukrainian crews were very proficient in the loading, sighting and firing process.

When they finally ended their training at 1600 hours the training sergeant told them all to go back to their quarters, get changed into their PE shorts and tee-shirts and bathers and report to the heated Olympic Pool.

When they all reported to the pool the instructor ordered them all to enjoy some swimming and water exercises.

Some of the young men and women couldn't swim because they'd come from cold, land locked villages, so they were ordered to take in float noodles to ensure their safety.

It was a happy, enjoyable experience and they were all laughing and splashing about having a relaxing time in the warm water.

The next morning, they were all up at 0600 for a three kilometre run around the base. Most of them were in fine, fit condition, especially the three females who admitted that they were avid joggers before the war.

After breakfast it was back to the simulators for another days' training. They were all keen and their target scores were improving exponentially. By the end of a weeks' training, they were ready to train in actual Leopard II tanks on the firing range.

An air of excitement pervaded the barracks as they dressed into their new khaki overalls, strapped on their sidearms and put on their helmets and onboard devices. Transport trucks conveyed them to the firing range. When they arrived, they got out of the trucks, were inspected and introduced to the tank ammunition, cannon rounds and belts of 7.62 machine gun rounds. They all assisted with the loading of the ammunition into the vehicles. The Drivers received instructions on board from the trainer in priming, starting and engaging gears and steering. Soon seven tanks in the lines roared into life. Plumes of black smoke shot out of the exhaust at the rear of the tanks.

"If you need to escape from the tank in an emergency, this hatch located behind the driver's seat will allow you to do so. There are three extinguishers on board in case of fire," said the instructor.

"What do we do if we are struck by a missile?" asked Vasily.

"That's easily, you kiss your ass goodbye. These things usually blow up killing everyone on board," he warned.

Their faces dropped when he said this, but he wasn't joking. They had all been in active combat and fully realised the consequences of being inside exploding tanks and the fate of the occupants.

The three female trainees proved to be just as able, if not more so, than their male counterparts. Kayla, a sprightly redhead, emerged as the most skilful of the tank commanders with the highest target ratio of the entire cohort. They practised manoeuvres for three consecutive weeks and blew up targets of old sheds, vehicles and mocked up buildings. They were developing into a cohesive, effective attack force.

Digital sights helped pinpoint exact targets while onboard radar and computers fed them information that was hidden from the naked eye. Beyond Horizon distance vision proved to be a great asset and they couldn't wait to employ it in actual theatres of war.

After eight weeks of intensive training and team bonding, the squad was ready to march out and return with their Leopard II tanks to the war. Another training squad would arrive soon to undergo their training at the facility.

At the passing out parade they marched in full dress uniform with bright blue berets and yellow lanyards. They marched in tank crews, all twenty-eight of them.

As they assembled and dressed off, the Colonel of the training facility, a tall German officer, inspected them and pinned on their cavalry insignia. He saluted each one of them. Milo felt very proud as he took the salute.

That night the army transport vehicle drove them in to Berlin to celebrate. As he dropped them off at the beerhalls, the sergeant called to them,

"Don't get too drunk, your country needs you safe and well. Be back at base by 0700 in the morning!"

"Let's hit the grog!" said Vasily.

"I want to eat first," said Milo heading off towards the 'Das Lokal,' restaurant.

As they went in, Milo, Vasily, Vincent and Ilya were shown to a fancy table by the maitre de.

"Would you prefer a drink first while you peruse the menu gentlemen?" he asked."Yes! Four lagers please," said Vincent, taking the lead.

They made their selections, and were served by the most beautiful blonde waitress with big gorgeous, blue eyes.

She smiled and welcomed them,

"My name is Kirsten," she said in English, spoken with a German accent.

"I'll be serving your meals tonight, gentlemen."

Milo's, and Kirsten's eyes met and there was instant attraction between them. The others attempted to flirt with her and say funny things and she was polite and friendly towards them, but she kept returning to Milo. He was flattered by her attention but was troubled by pangs of guilt when he thought of Svetlana.

As the night went on the others drifted away and hooked up with other lovely women, leaving Milo at the table by himself, staring into the dancing light of the candles.

Soon Milo found himself sadly drinking alone. Kirsten noticed him and came over and sat beside him.

"I've finished, duty now Milo. Would you care to walk me home? I can show you the Brandenburg Gate on the way," she offered.

"How far away do you live Kirsten?" he asked.

"About five blocks," she answered.

Milo walked along beside her in the cool Berlin night. She wore only her waitress uniform and a light cardigan, so Milo took off his jacket and placed it around her shoulders. She had a way of making him feel so special and was so nice to be with. Her perfume, he later learnt, was called, "Obsession," wafted into his senses and hypnotised him.

"There's the Brandenburg Gate, just off the Pariser Platz," she said.

There were six floodlit columns holding up a gigantic arch with the statue of a chariot on top of it. It was a magnificent old historical structure.

Milo stood admiring it and put his arms around Kirsten and kissed her hair, breathing in her unique scent. After a while they walked on and he held her hand, stepping along the ancient cobblestones and enjoying the fondness of being with her. They talked as they walked along and became very fond of each other as they went. Finally, they reached the steps of her apartment as the clock struck twelve.

"Oh Milo, I've so enjoyed you walking me home and showing you my home city. It's been such a wonderful evening."

"Kirsten, there something I must tell say," he said, sadly.

"That you're married! I already know. You're wearing a wedding ring," she commented.

"I'm sorry if I've misled you," he told her.

"Don't be silly. If I can have you for just a while, it's much better than not having you at all," she said, as a tear ran down her cheek.

"Svetlana is a nurse in Kyiv, she attends the wounded from the war,' he told her.

"I don't care. She's not here, she isn't giving you the love you deserve tonight, Milo. Please let me show you how much I can love you," she implored.

"I don't know if I could do that to her," he argued weakly.

"Well at least come up and have a cup of coffee with me. Surely, that's not too much to ask?" she entreated.

"Okay! A coffee between friends should be fine," he agreed.

They ascended the stairs and the door opened into a beautifully furnished apartment. She sat him down and loosened his tie. She folded his jacket and placed it over a chair then went to put the jug on for the coffee.

When she came back with the coffee she put on some soft music and sat down beside him. They spoke quietly and she wove a web of charm around Milo that enraptured his complete attention.

Kirsten leaned her lovely head on his broad shoulder and kicked off her shoes. The sweet perfume of her carried his senses away. After a while they were kissing passionately and being healthy young people, they were locked in a loving embrace.

Suddenly, he stopped kissing and said, "I shouldn't be doing this."

"We shouldn't be doing this! There shouldn't be a war! You shouldn't be married!" she said, emphatically, "We are entitled to one night of love Milo. Nobody will ever know or care.

You could be killed, and you will have died never knowing my love. Go with it, Milo. You can't be a hero saving everyone else and sacrificing yourself," she said.

Milo capitulated and gave Kirsten all his love.

"She's right," he thought to himself, "We only live once."

Kirsten was everything she'd promised to be, and they made love repeatedly. When they finally slept, it was the peaceful sleep of requited love. Nothing existed but the present, and the present was all that there was.

In spite of a night of bliss, Milo was up, dressed and calling for a taxi at 0500 to take him back to the military base.

As he kissed Kirsten goodbye, they both wondered if they'd ever be seeing each other again. Milo gave her his cell phone number and asked her to call him sometime. They embraced one final passionate time then he could hear the taxi beckoning. Reluctantly he scrambled down the stairs to the street and he was gone.

"You certainly disappeared last night. How did you get on with that lovely waitress?" asked Vincent.

"We went for a walk to the Brandenburg Gate," Milo told him.

"Wow! You must have walked a long way, comrade, it's taken you all night to get back," said Vincent.

"Sh!" said Milo, putting his finger up to his lips.

At 1200 hours they boarded the transport plane and flew back to Kyiv. The Leopard II tanks would be brought to Ukraine on flat top rail cars and would arrive within a week's time of their return.

When the Leopard tanks arrived in Ukraine and were reunited with their trained crews, they became valuable assets to the defending battle groups. In action they proved to be extremely effective.

Milo's crew saw a number of engagements and always emerged victorious. The new tanks were an excellent boost to morale for the fighting soldiers and artillery.

The tide of the war began to turn gradually in favour of the defenders.

Milo sat with the crew discussing the mornings' operations when a radio communication came through,

"Tank Commander Milosovic, I have some rather sad news for you. Unfortunately, your wife, Svetlana, has been killed in a drone attack on the hospital in Kyiv. We can only tell you that she, and fifteen of her colleagues were on duty when the drone devastated the emergency ward. She is to be buried in the Kyiv Memorial Cemetery."

Milo's heart sank as he imagined her final moments as tears came to his eyes.

"Oh Lana, this so terrible!" he thought to himself.

Vincent asked him what had happened, but he seemed to be in a suspended dream and didn't answer.

He went to his NCO and told him what had happened, but he said that leave was impossible at this phase of operations.

"You'll just have to keep on fighting at this time comrade. We can't do without you,' he said.

Milo believed that his heart would break, especially when he recalled his recent infidelity with Kirsten.

That evening, during stand down he drowned his sorrow with vodka and surprised his comrades who had never seen him drunk before. When he did wake up, he wished he hadn't and his head ached as if he'd been shot in the skull. After he'd showered and eaten, he went on duty and was surprised that he was beginning to feel better. His tank crew and his country needed him and he wasn't about to let them down. He led them well and that day, despite his personal loss, they destroyed three Russian tanks and an armoured personnel carrier.

At the end of the month he was granted leave and immediately phoned Kirsten to tell her that he was coming to Berlin and that he would like to see her.

They talked on the cell phone, and he explained what had happened to his wife.

"I'm sorry to hear that Milo, but please remember that I love you and I will do my best to make you happy again," she told him.

When they did meet again they fell into each other's arms and cried.

"She wanted to do her duty to her country, and it ended up taking her life," said Milo, "We had actually left Ukraine and gone to Finland and were safe. Svetlana wanted us to go back. I wasn't sure. I'm tired of all the killing."

"You can come here and live in Berlin. You don't have to give your life for your country. You are better off alive, rather than a dead hero buried in some distant cemetery," she told him.

Milo decided then and there to leave the army and the war. He would seek asylum in Germany and see if he could get work as a computer technician.

He went to see the Red Cross and the German Embassy. The Ukrainians pleaded with him to go back but he was diagnosed with PTSD and said that he could no longer participate in the war.

The Red Cross assisted him, and the German Embassy granted him asylum and refugee status. He was safe from Ukrainian officials pursuing him to get him to go back and fight.

Gradually, Kirsten and Milo established their relationship and he found work in the Berlin computer industry repairing and providing technical service to individuals. Kirsten continued her work as a waitress at 'Das Lokal,' and life settled down into a comfortable routine.

When Yuri phoned him, he was astounded by the information Milo related. He was shocked to learn that Svetlana had died in Kyiv and that Milo had left the army, and Ukraine and gone to live with Kirsten in Berlin. Everything had changed. He told Milo about the KGB agents visiting Grandfather Peter and of how they should have been more careful with such a skilful, independent individual.

During their conversation they both vowed to get back together again.

"I would love to introduce you to our son, Peter. Perhaps you two would consent to becoming his Godparents?" asked Yuri.

When the phone call concluded Milo and Kirsten sat together on the big lounge drinking coffee.

"It's very sad what happened to Svetlana but I hope that I can love you enough to make our life here together everything you would like it to be. Also, I have some news for you Milo. We are going to have a baby, Darling," she announced.

"That's wonderful," said Milo smiling at her.

He took her in his arms and kissed her.

"And we will be the best parents ever," he said.

A while later a news flash came onto their television screen,

"Russian missile attacks have been directed towards all Ukraine's major cities in retribution for strategic military failures throughout the country," the presenter announced.

"It just keeps going on doesn't it, Milo," said Kirsten.

"I don't think it's ever going to end," said Milo, switching off the television.

www.ingramcontent.com/pod-product-compliance
Lightning Source LLC
Chambersburg PA
CBHW030822200726
48288CB00004B/1349